THE USBORNE

FIRST THOUSAND WORDS

IN ARABIC

With easy pronunciation guide

Heather Amery

Illustrated by Stephen Cartwright

Arabic language consultant: Adi Budeiri

Editor: Lisa Watts; Designer (revised edition): Andy Griffin

Translation and typesetting by y2ktranslations and Mouna Hammad

On every double page with pictures,
there is a little yellow duck to look for.
Can you find it?

About this book

This book provides a fun and engaging way for beginners to learn Arabic. On most of the pages, large, colorful panoramic scenes are surrounded with small pictures labeled with their names in Arabic.

Saying the words

Each Arabic word is also written in Roman letters, to show you how to pronounce it. Reading the words while looking at the pictures will help you remember them, and you can test yourself by looking for and naming the objects in the panoramic scenes. You can even practice forming simple sentences to talk about the pictures.

Arabic alphabet

At the back of the book there is a guide to the Arabic alphabet and a list of all the Arabic words with their pronunciation guides and meanings in English. Arabic is written from right to left and there are several sounds for which there are no equivalents in English. The pronunciation guides will help you, but the best way to learn how to say the words is to listen to a native Arabic speaker.

المنزل

el-manzil

مغطس
maghtas

صابون
saboon

حنفيّة
hanafiyya

ورق حمّام
waraq hammam

فُرشة أسنان
furshat asnan

ماء
ma'

مرحاض
mirhad

سفنجة
sfinja

مغسلة
maghsaleh

دوش
doosh

منشفة
manshafa

سرير
sareer

حمّام
hammam

صالون
salon

معجون أسنان
ma''joun asnan

راديو
radio

مخدة
makhada

قُرص مُدمج
qurs mudmaj

سجادة
sujjada

كنبة
kanabay

4

كُرسي
kursi

لحاف
lihaf

مُشط
musht

شَرشَف
sharshaf

بساطة
bisata

خزانة
khazana

مخدة نوم
makhadat nawm

غرفة نوم
ghurfat nawm

خزانة جوارير
khazanat jawareer

مِرآة mir'a

فُرشة شَعر
furshat sha"r

قِنديل
qandeel

مَدخَل
madkhal

مُلصقات
mulsaqat

علاقة
"allaqa

هاتف
hatef

راديتير
radiatur

مُسجّل فيديو
musajjel video

جَريدة
jareeda

طاولة
tawila

رَسائل
rasa'el

درج
daraj

5

المطبخ
el matbakh

ثلاجة thallaja

أكواب akwab

ساعة حائط sa''at ha'et

سكملة skamla

معالق صغيرة ma''alleq sagheera

مفتاح الكهرباء miftah el kahraba

مسحوق غسيل mas-houq ghaseel

مفتاح miftah

باب baab

مغسلة maghsaleh

مكنسة كهربائية mukunsa kahraba'eya

طناجر tanaajer

شُوَك shuwak

مريول maryool

طاولة الكوي tawilat el kawi

زبالة zibala

إبريق غلي
ibreeq ghali

سكاكين
sakakeen

مكنسة خشنة
mukunsa khashina

خرقة
khirqa

بلاط صيني
balat sini

مكنسة
mukunsa

غسالة
ghassaleh

مجرود
majrood

جرار
jarrar

صحون صغيرة
suhoun sagheera

مقلاة
maqla

فرن
furun

ملاعق خشب
mala"eq khashab

صحون
suhoun

مكواة
mikwa

خزانة حائط
khazanat ha'et

ممسحة
mamsaha

فناجين
fanajeen

علبة كبريت
"ulbat kibrit

فرشة
fursha

طاسات
tasat

7

البستان

el bustan

عربة يد
"arabet yad

خلية نحل
khaliyat nahel

حلزون
halazoon

طوب
toob

حمامة
hamama

مجرفة
majrafa

أم علي
um "ali

زبالة
zibala

بزر
bizr

كوخ
kukh

مرش
mirrash

دودة أرض
dudet ard

أزهار
azhar

رشاش ماء
rashash ma'

مجرفة
majrafa

دبور
dabbour

8

نحلة
nahla

مسطرين
mastareen

عظمة
"athma

سياج
siyaj

شوكة
shawka

مقص الحشيش
miqass el hasheesh

ممر
mammar

أوراق شجر
awraq shajar

شجرة
shajara

دخان
dukhan

دودة
dudah

مشط
musht

عش
"ush

عصى
"usy

بيت بلاستيك
beit plastik

أعشاب
a"shab

عربة أطفال
"arabat atfal

سلم
sullam

نار
nar

أنبوب سقي
anboob saqi

الورشة
el warsha

ملزمة
malzama

ورق زجاج
waraq zujaj

مقدح
miqdah

سلم
sullam

منشار
munshar

نشارة
nishara

تقويم
taqweem

صندوق عدة
sundouq "idda

براغي صغيرة
baraghi sagheera

مفك
mafak

لوح خشب
lawh khashab

نجارة
nijara

موس
moose

مسامير رسم
masameer rasem

عنكبوت
"ankaboot

براغي
baraghi

صوامل
sawameel

نسيج عنكبوت
naseej "ankaboot

برميل
barmeel

ذبابة
thubaba

بلطة
balta

متر
mitr

مطرقة
mitraqa

مبرد
mabrad

علبة دهان
"ulbat dihan

فارة
fara

قطع خشب
qita" khashab

مسامير
masameer

جحش نجارة jahsh nijara

مرطبانات
martabanat

دكان
dukkan

حفرة
hufra

مقهى
maqha

سيارة إسعاف
sayyarat is"af

رصيف
raseef

هوائي
hawa'ee

مدخنة
madkhana

سقف
saqf

جرافة
jarrafa

فندق
funduq

الشارع
ish-share"

حافلة
hafila

رجل
rajul

سيارة الشرطة
sayyarat esh-shurta

أنابيب
anabeeb

حفارة
haffara

مدرسة
madrasa

ملعب
mal"ab

12

سيارة أجرة
sayyarat ujra

ممر مشاة
mammar musha

مصنع
masna"

شاحنة
shahina

إشارات ضوئية
isharat daw'iya

دار السينما
dar is-sinema

سيارة شحن
sayyarat shahn

مدحلة
midhala

عربة
"araba

دار
dar

سوق
souq

درج
daraj

دراجة نارية
darraja nariya

بناية binaya

دراجة
darraja

سيارة الإطفاء
sayyarat el itfa'

شرطي
shurti

سيارة
sayyara

إمرأة
imra'a

عامود إنارة
"amood inara

13

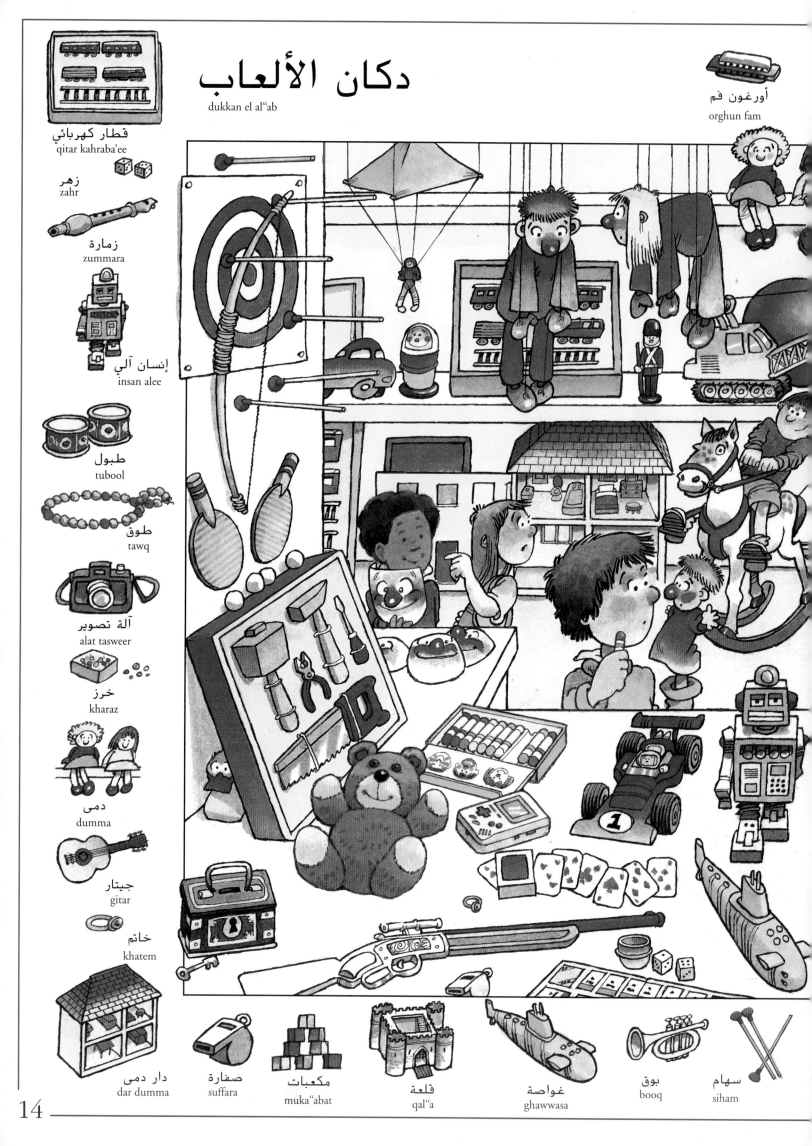

دكان الألعاب
dukkan el al"ab

أورغون فم
orghun fam

قطار كهربائي
qitar kahraba'ee

زهر
zahr

زمارة
zummara

إنسان آلي
insan alee

طبول
tubool

طوق
tawq

آلة تصوير
alat tasweer

خرز
kharaz

دمى
dumma

جيتار
gitar

خاتم
khatem

دار دمى
dar dumma

صفارة
suffara

مكعبات
muka"abat

قلعة
qal"a

غواصة
ghawwasa

بوق
booq

سهام
siham

قوس
qaws

مظلة هبوط
mithalat huboot

مركب شراعي
markab shira"i

أصابع ألوان
asabe" alwan

مدحلة
midhala

أقنعة
aqni"a

سيارة سباق
sayyarat sibaq

حصان هزاز
hisan hazzaz

حصالة
hassala

غلل
ghulal

عرائس
"ara'es

بيانو
piano

رواد فضاء
ruwwad fada'

رافعة
rafi"a

ملتينة
malteenah

بندقية
bunduqiyya

جنود معدنية
junood ma"daniya

صندوق ألوان
sandooq alwan

صاروخ
sarookh

الحديقة العامة
el hadeeqa el "amma

مراجيح
marajeeh

حوض رمل
hawd raml

نزهة
nuzha

طيارة ورق
tayyarat waraq

بوظة
bootha

كلب
kalb

حاجز
hajez

طريق
tareeq

ضفدع
dufda"

مزلقة
mizlaqa

مقعد
maq"ad

فرخ الضفضع
farkh ed-dufda"

بحيرة
buhaira

أحذية تزلج
ahthiyat tazzaluj

عشبة
"ushba

رضيع
radee"

لوحة نزلج
lawhat tazzluj

تراب
turab

عربة أطفال
"arabat atfal

زحلوقة
zahlouka

أطفال
atfal

دراجة ثلاثية
darraja thulathiya

عصافير
"asafeer

سياج
siyaj

كرة
kura

قارب
qareb

خيطان
khitan

بريكة
burreika

فرخ البط
farkh el batt

حبل القفز
habl elqafz

شجر
shajar

حوض زريعة
hawd zira"a

وز
waz

رسن
rasan

بط
batt

17

حديقة الحيوانات
hadiqat el-hayawanat

بندا
panda

جناح
janah

صقر
saqr

جاموس البحر
jamoos el-bahr

قرد
qird

خفاش
khaffash

غوريلا
ghorilla

كفوف
kufuf

قنغر
kanghur

ذنب
thanab

ذئب
th'ib

صخرة جليد
sakhrat jaleed

بطريق
batreeq

دب
dub

ريش
reesh

تمساح
timsah

بجع
baja"

نعامة
na"ama

دلفين
dolfin

أسد
asad

أشبال
ashbal

زرافة
zarafa

18

قُرون
quroon

أيِّل
ayl

جمل
jamal

فقمة
faqama

دب قطبي
dub qutbi

سلحفاة
sulhafa

خرطوم
khurtoom

كَركَدن
karkadan

فيل
feel

ثور أمريكي
thawr amreki

سمور
sammour

حمار الوحش
himar el wahsh

حية
hayya

ماعز
ma''ez

سمك قرش
samak qirsh

حوت
hoot

نمر
nimer

فهد
fahed

19

السفر
es-safar

طائرة عامودية
ta'ira "amoodiya

سكة حديد
sikkat hadeed

قاطرة
qatira

مصيد
musidd

عربات النقل
"arabat en-naql

مكانيكي
mikaniki

قطار البضائع
qitar el bada'e"

رصيف
raseef

مراقبة
muraqiba

حقيبة
haqiba

آلة التذاكر
'alat et-tathakir

محطة القطار
mahatat el qitar

المرآب
el mar'ab

إشارات ضوئية
isharat daw'iya

حقيبة الظهر
haqibat eth-thaher

أضواء أمامية
adwa' amamiya

محرك
muharik

عجلة
"ajala

بطارية
battariya

طائرة
ta'ira

مضيفة
mudeefa

مدرّج
mudarraj

برج المراقبة
burj el muraqaba

المطار
el mattar

مضيف
mudeef

طيار
tayyar

مغسلة سيّارات
maghsalat sayyarat

صندوق
sundooq

بنزين
banzeen

مغسلة سيارات

سيّارة تصليح
sayyarat tasleeh

مضخّة البنزين
madakhat el banzeen

شاحنة صهريج
shahinat sahreej

مفتاح
miftah

إطار مطّاط
itar mattat

غطاء المُحرّك
ghita' el muharik

زيت
zayt

مُحَرِك هوائي
muharik hawa'ee

منطاد
mintad

فراشة
farasha

سحلية
suhliya

حِجارَة
hijara

ثعلب
tha"lab

جدول
jadwal

عمود الإتجاهات
"amood el ittijahat

قنفذ
qunfud

الريـف
er-reef

جبل
jabal

حابس
habis

سنجاب
sinjab

غابة
ghaba

غُرَير
ghurair

نهر
nahr

طريق
tareeq

22

خيام
khiyam

قناة
qana

جذوع الشجر
juthoo" esh-shajar

قَرية
qarya

فَراشة ليل
farashat layl

جسر
jisr

مركب بضائع
markab bada'e"

شلاّل
shallal

بومة
booma

نفق
nafaq

جرو الثعلب
jarou eth-tha"lab

خُلند
khlund

صيّاد سمَك
sayyad samak

صخور
sukhoor

ضفضعتين
dufda"teen

قطار
qitar

بيت منقول
bayt manqool

تَلّة
talla

23

متبنة
matbaneh

كلب الراعي
kalb er-ra"i

بط
batt

حملان
humlan

بركة
birka

صيصان
seesan

مخزن القمح
makhzan el qamh

حظيرة الخنازير
hatherat el khanazeer

ثور
thawr

فرخ البط
farkh el batt

قن دجاج
qunn dajaj

جرارة
jarrara

المزرعة
el mazra"a

ديك
deek

أوزات
awzat

شاحنة صهريج
shahinat sahreej

حظيرة
hatheera

وحل
wahl

عربة
"araba

مزارع muzare"
حقل haql
دجاج dajaj
عجل "ijl
سياج siyaj
سرج sarj
حظيرة بقر hatherat baqar

بقرة baqara

محراث mihrath

بستان فاكهة bustan fakiha

إسطبل istabel

خنانيص khananees

راعية ra"iya

ديوك حبش duyuk habash

فزاعة fazza"a

مزرعة mazra"a

حشيش hasheesh
خرفان khirfan
حزم التبن huzam et-tibn
حصان hissan
خنازير khanazeer

صدفة
sadafa

مركب شراعي
markab shira"i

بحر
bahr

مجداف
mijdaf

منار
manar

مجرفة
mijrafa

سطل
sattel

نجمة البحر
najmat el bahr

قلعة رملية
qal"a ramliya

شمسية
shamsiya

علم
"alam

بحّار
bahhar

سرطان
saratan

نورس
nawras

جزيرة
jazeera

قارب سريع
qareb saree"

نزلّج مائي
tazalluj ma'ee

أمواج
amwaj

قبعة القش
quba"at el-qash

جرف
jurf

سفينة
safeena

زورق
zawraq

حبل
habl

حصى
hasa

طحالب
tahaleb

شبكة
shabaka

مجداف
mijdaf

قارب صيد
qareb sayd

زعانف
za"anef

حمار
himar

سمك
samak

لباس سباحة
libas sibaha

ناقلة نفط
naqilat naft

شاطيء
shate'

زورق
zawraq

كرسي مركب
kursi markab

المدرسة

el madrasa

مِقَصّ
miqass

٢+٢=٤
٣+٢=٥

حِسَاب
hisab

مِمحاة
mimha

مِسطرة
mistara

صُوَر
suwar

أقلام لبدية
aqlam labbadiya

مسامير رسم
masameer rasem

صندوق ألوان
sandooq alwan

وَلَد
walad

قلَم حبرجاف
qalam hiber jaf

لوح
lawh

مكتب
maktab

كُتُب
kutub

قلَم حبر
qalam hiber

غِراء
ghira'

طباشير
tabashir

رسم
rasm

28

سلّة المهملات
sallat el muhmalat

مُدَرِّسة
mouderissa

صندوق
sandooq

خريطة
kharita

ريشة
risha

سقَف
saqf

حائط
ha'et

أرضية
ardiyya

دَفتَر
daftar

ألِفباء
alefba'

شارة
shara

حوض سمك
hawd samak

ورَق
waraq

ستار
sitar

لوح أسود
lawh aswad

فنديل
qandeel

ألوان شمع
alwan shame"

بنت
bint

كرة أرضية
kura ardiyya

نبته
nabta

يد الباب
yad el bab

29

المُستَشفى
el mustashfa

مُمَرِّض
mumarred

قُطن
qutun

دواء
dawa'

مِصعَد
mis"ad

روب
roob

عكازات
"akkazat

أقراص
aqras

صينية
seniya

ساعة يَدّ
sa"at yad

ميزان حرارة
mizan harara

ستار
sitar

دب
dub

تُفاحة
tuffaha

جبارة
jibara

ضماد
dimad

كُرسي نقّال
kursi naqqal

لعبة أحجية
lu"bat uhjiah

طبيبة
tabeeba

إبرة
ibra

30

الطَّبيب
el tabeeb

شبشب
shibsheb

حاسوب
hasoob

ضماد لاصق
dimad laseq

موز
mawz

عنب
"inab

سلّة
salla

ألعاب
al"ab

أجاص
ajas

بطاقات
bitaqat

حفاض
hifad

عصا
"asa

قاعة الإنتظار
qa"at el intithar

تلفزيون
televizyon

قميص نوم
qamees nawm

لباس نوم
libas nawm

برتقالة
burtqala

مناديل ورق
manadeel waraq

رواية مصورة
riwaya mussawara

31

الحَفلة

el hafla

هدايا
hadaya

بالون
balloon

شوكولاتة
shokolata

ملبس
mlabass

نافذة
nafitha

ألعاب نارية
al"ab nariyya

وِشَاح
wishah

كَعكَة
ka"ka

مصاصة
massasa

شَمعَة
sham"a

ورق زينة
waraq zena

ألعَاب
al"ab

ماندالينة
mandalina

سُجُق
sujuq

شَريط مُسَجّل
shareet mussajel

نَقانَق
naqaneq

شرائح البَطاطا
shara'eh el batata

أزياء تَنَكُرية
azya' tannakuriyya

كرز
karaz

عَصير فَواكِه
'aseer fawakih

توت
toot

فَراولة
farawla

لمبة
lamba

غطاء الطاولة
ghita' et-tawila

شَطيرة
shateera

زُبدَة
zubda

بِسكوت
baskoot

جبنة
jubna

خبز
khubz

البقالة
el baqqala

غرابفروت
grapefroot

جَزَر
jazar

قَرنبيط
qarnabeet

كُراث
kurath

فِطر
fitr

خِيار
khiyar

ليمون
laimoon

كَرَفْس
karafs

مشمش
mishmish

بَطيخ
batteekh

حقيبة
haqeeba

جبنة

خضر وفواكه

بَصَل
basal

ملفوف
malfoof

خوخ
khookh

خسّ
khass

بزيلا
bazilla

بندورة
bandoura

بيض
bayd

برقوق
barqooq

طحين
taheen

ميزان
mizan

مرطبانات
martabanat

لحمة
lahma

أناناس
ananas

لبن رائب
laban ra'eb

سلّة
salla

زُجاجات
zujajat

حقيبة يد
haqibat yad

كيس نقود
kees nqood

نُقود
nuqood

مُعلّبات
mu"allabat

عربة
"araba

بَطاطا
batata

سبانخ
sabanekh

فاصولية
fasoolya

صَندوق الدفع
sundooq ed-daf"

قَرع
qar"

الأكل
el akl

غذاء
ghatha'

فطور
futoor

بيض مسلوق
bayd maslooq

خُبز مُحمَّص
khubz muhamas

مُربّى
murabba

قهوة
qahwa

بيض مقلى
bayd maqli

قِشدَة
qishda

حَليب
haleeb

حبوب
huboob

شوكولاته ساخنة
shokolata sakhina

سُكَّر
sukkar

عَسَل
'asal

ملح
malh

فلفل
filfil

شاي
shay

إبريق شاي
ibreeq shay

فطائر
fata'er

أقراص خبز
aqras khubz

36

عَشاء
"asha"

لَحمة
lahma

شوربة
shoraba

عُجّة
"ujja

عصي
"usi

سَلَطة
salata

برغر
burger

دجاجة
dajaja

صلصة بندورة
salsat bandoura

أرُز
arruz

معكرونة
ma"karona

بطاطا مهروسة
batata mahroosa

بتزة
pitza

بطاطا مقلية
batata maqliyya

تحليَات
tahliyat

أنا
ana

رأس
ra's

شَعَر
sha"r

وَجه
wajh

حاجب
hajib

عَين
"ayn

أُنف
anf

ذراع
thira"

كوع
koo"

بَطن
batn

خَد
khadd

فَم
famm

شِفاه
shiffah

أسنان
asnan

لِسان
lisan

ذَقن
thaqn

أذن
uthn

رقبة
raqaba

كَتف
katef

أصابع الرِجل
asabe" ar-rijil

رِجل
rijel

سَاق
saq

رُكبة
rukba

صَدر
sadr

ظَهر
thaher

خَلف
khalf

يَدّ
yad

إبهام
ibham

أصابع
asabe"

مَلبس
malbas

جوارب jawareb	سِروال داخلي sirwal dakhili	قميص شباح qamees shabbah	سِروال sirwal	جينز jeens	قميص داخلي qamees dakhili
تنّورة tannoura	قميص qamees	رباط عنق rabbat "unq	سروال قصير sirwal qaseer	جراب طويل jirab taweel	فستان fustan
كَنزة صوف kanzat soof	قميص qamees	سترة صوف sutrat soof	لفحة lafha		منديل mandeel
أحذية رياضة ahthiyat riyada	أحذية ahthiya	صندل sandal	جزمة jazma		كفوف kufoof
	حِزام hizam	إبزيم i'bzeem	سحَاب sahhab	رباط rabbat	زرّ zirr
جيوب juyub	معطف mi"taf	سُترة sutra	طاقية taqiya		عُروة "urwa
					قبعة qubba"a

39

الناس

مُمَثِّل
mumathel

مُمَثِّلة
mumathela

طَبَّاخ
tabbakh

راقِص
raqes

راقِصة
raqisa

مُغَنِّي
mughani

مغنية
mughaniya

رائد فضاء
ra'ed fada'

لحّام
lahham

رجال الشرطة/ نساء الشرطة
rijal esh-shurta / nisa' esh-shurta

نَجّار
najjar

رجُل إطفاء
rajul itfa'

فنانة
fannana

قاضي
qadi

ميكانيكي
mikaniki

ميكانيكية
mikanikiya

سائِقة شاحنة
sa'eqat shahina

قائد حافلة
qa'ed hafila

حلاق
hallaq

طبيبة أسنان
tabeebat asnan

غواص
ghawwas

نَادِل
nadel

نادِلة
nadila

ساعي البَريد
sa"i el bareed

دهان
dahhan

خبّازة
khabbaza

العائلة
al "a'ila

إبن
ibn

أخ
akh

إبنة
ibna

أُخت
ukht

أُم
umm

زوجة
zawja

أب
abb

زوج
zawj

عمّة "amma
خالة khala

عمّ "amm
خال khal

إبن عمّ ibn "amm
إبن خال ibn khal

جدّ
jadd

جدّة
jadda

الأعمال اليومية

el a"mal el yawmiyah

إبتسام
ibtisam

بكاء
buka'

تفكير
tafkeer

سمع
sama"

ضحك
dahk

قبض
qabd

رمي
ramy

كسر
kasr

رسم
rasm

كتابة
kitaba

قطع
qat"

قص
qass

أكل
akl

تكلم
takkalum

حفر
hafr

حمل
haml

شرب
shurb

صنع
sun"

قفز
qafz

زحف
zahf

رقص
raqs

غسل
ghasl

حباكة
hiyaka

مُشاهدة
mushahada

تسلُق
tassalluq

لعب
lu"b

أخذ
akhth

قفز بالحبل
qafz bil habl

شِجار
shijar

نوم
nawm

خِياطة
khiyata

إنتظار
intithar

إختباء
ikhtiba'

قراءة
qira'a

شراء
shira'

طبخ
tabkh

دَفع
daf"

غِناء
ghina'

نفخ
nafkh

شَدّ
shadd

كنس
kans

قطف
qatf

سقوط
suqoot

مشي
mashy

ركض
rakd

جلوس
juloos

43

الأضداد

el ad-daad

جيد
jayyid

سيء
say-yi'

بعيد
ba"eed

قريب
qareeb

فوق
fawq

بارد
bared

ساخن
sakhen

مبلّل
muballal

جاف
jaf

تحت
taht

على
"ala

وسَخ
wasikh

نَظيف
natheef

تحت
taht

سمين
sameen

نحيف
naheef

صغير
sagheer

كبير
kabeer

مفتوح
maftouh

مغلق
mughlaq

قليل
qaleel

كَثير
katheer

أوّل
awwal

أخير
akheer

يسار
yasar

44

خارج
kharij

داخل
dakhel

سهل
sahl

صَعب
sa"b

فارغ
farigh

مليء
malee'

رخو
rakh-w

قاسٍ
qasi

أمام
amam

عالٍ
"ali

بطيء
batee'

سريع
saree"

وراء
wara'

واطيء
wate'

طويل
taweel

قصير
qaseer

ميت
mayyit

حيّ
hayy

معتم
mu"tem

مُضيء
mudee'

قديم
qadeem

عالٍ
"ali

يمين
yameen

جَديد
jadeed

واطيء
wate'

الأيـام
el ayyam

الأَحَد
el-ahad

الخميس
el-khamees

الثُلاثاء
eth-thulatha'

الأربعاء
el-arbi"a'

السبت
es-sabt

الإثنين
el-ithnayn

الجمعة
ej-jum"a

تقويم
taqweem

نهار
nahar

مساء
masa'

شمس
shams

ليل
layl

قمر
qamar

نجمة
najma

فضاء
fada'

كوكب
kawkab

سفينة فضاء
safinat fada'

منظار
minthar

46

الأعياد
el-a"yad

عيد ميلاد
"eed milad

بطاقات عيد ميلاد
bitaqat "eed milad

شمعة
sham"a

عطلة
"utla

هدية
hadiyya

كعكة عيد ميلاد
ka"kat "eed milad

يوم الزفاف
yawm ez-zafaf

آلة تصوير
alat tasweer

وصيفة
waseefa

عروس
"aroos

عريس
"arees

مصور
musawwir

عيد الميلاد
"eed el milad

أيل
ayl

بابا نويل
baba nowel

زلاجة
zallaja

شجرة عيد الميلاد
shajarat "eed el milad

أحوال الطقس

ahwal et-taqs

شمس
shams

غيوم
ghuyum

سماء
sama'

مظلة
mithala

مطر
matar

برق
barq

سديم
sediim

ثلج
thalj

ندى
nada

ريح
reeh

ضباب
dabaab

جليد
jaleed

قوس قزح
qaws quzah

الفصول

el fusool

ربيع
rabee"

صيف
sayf

خريف
khareef

شتاء
shita'

حيوانات أليفة
hayawanat aleefa

بيطرية
baytariyya

مرنب
marnab

بيت الكلب
bayt el kalb

بودغريغر
budgerigar

خنزير هندي
khanzeer hindi

كلب
kalb

جرو
jaru

أكل
akl

بيغاء
babbagha'

منقار
munqar

كنار
kinar

قفص
qafas

أرنب
arnab

هرة
hirra

سلّة
salla

فار
fa'r

هريرة
huraira

حليب
haleeb

سمك ذهبي
samak thahabee

الرياضة
er-riyadha

كُرة السلة
kurat es-sallah

تجديف
tajdeef

لوحة تزلج
lawhat tazalluj

إبحارشراعي
ibhar shira"i

لوحة شـراعية
lawha shira"iyya

كريكت
kriket

مضرب
madrab

كُراتي
karate

كرة قدم أمريكية
kurat qadam amerikiya

جمباز
jumbaz

مضرب
madrab

كرة
kura

تنيس أرضي
tennis ardi

سنارة
sunnara

صيد سمك
sayd samak

طعم
tu"m

رقص
raqs

كرة القاعدة
kurat el qa"ida

رُغبي
rugby

غوص
ghaws

مسبح
masbah

سباحة
sibaha

سباق الركض
sibaq er-rakd

رمي بالقوس
ramy bil qaws

مرمى
marma

طيران شراعي
tayaran shira"i

خوذة
khootha

عدو
"ado

دراجات هوائية
darrajat haw'iyya

تسلق
tassalluq

خزانة حائط
khazanat ha'et

جودو
judo

حصان
hissan

فرس
faras

كرة القدم
kurat el-qadam

فروسية
furusiyya

غرفة غيار
ghurfat ghayar

كرة الريشة
kurat er-reesha

تنيس الطاولة
tennis et-tawila

مزالج جليد
mazalej jaleed

تزلج جليدي
tazalluj jaleedi

عصا تزلج
"asa tazalluj

مقعد هوائي
miq"ad hawa'ee

مزَالج
mazalej

تزَلج على الثلج
tazalluj "ala eth-thalj

مصارعة سومو
musar"at sumo

51

الألوان
el alwan

برتقالى
burtuqali

أخضر
akhdar

أسود
aswad

رمادي
ramadi

أحمر
ahmar

بنى
bunnee

أبيض
abyad

أزرق
azraq

وردي
wardi

بنفسجي
banafsaji

أصفر
asfar

الأشكال
el ashkal

مستطيل
mustateel

دائرة
da'era

معين
ma''een

مخروط
makhroot

نجمة
najma

مكعب
muka''ab

بيضي
baydi

مثلث
muthalath

مربع
murraba''

هلال
hilal

الأعداد
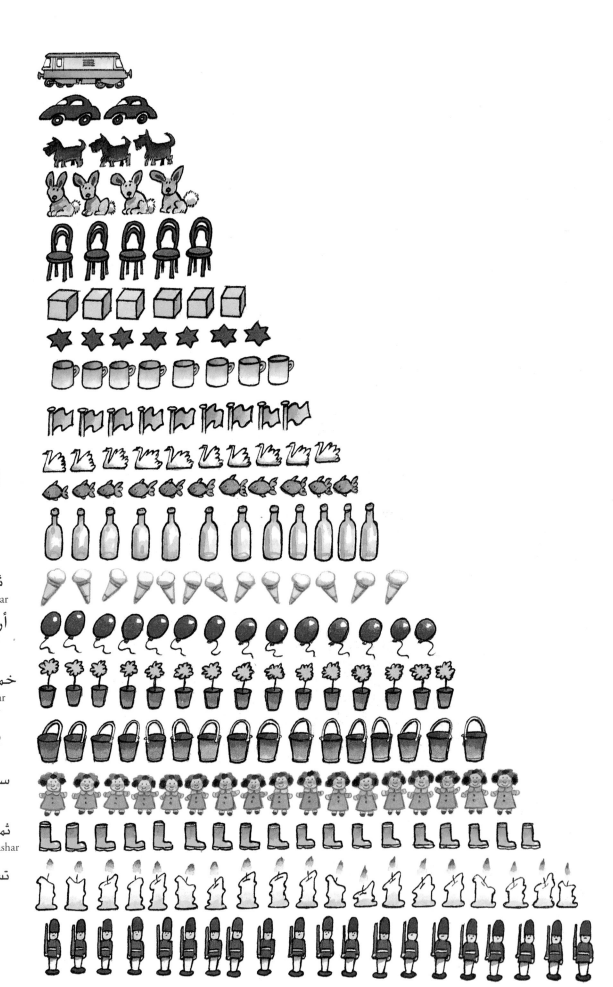

el a"dad

١	واحد wahid	
٢	إثنان ithnan	
٣	ثلاثة thalatha	
٤	أربعة arba"a	
٥	خمسة khamsa	
٦	ستة sitta	
٧	سبعة sab"a	
٨	ثمانية thamaniya	
٩	تسعة tis"a	
١٠	عشرة "ashara	
١١	أحد عشر ihada "ashar	
١٢	إثنا عشر ithna "ashar	
١٣	ثلاثة عشر thalathata "ashar	
١٤	أربعة عشر arba"ata "ashar	
١٥	خمسة عشر khamsata "ashar	
١٦	ستة عشر sittata "ashar	
١٧	سبعة عشر sab"ata "ashar	
١٨	ثمانية عشر thamaniyata "ashar	
١٩	تسعة عشر tis"ata "ashar	
٢٠	عشرون "ishroon	

53

مدينة الملاهي
madinat el malahi

دوارة
dawara

ممسحة أقدام
mamsahat aqdam

مزلقة عملاقة
mizlaqa "imlaqa

دولاب الكبير
doolab el kabeer

قطار الرعب
qitar er-ru"b

فشار
fushar

حلقات
halaqaat

جبال روسية
jibal roosiyya

رمي البندقية
ramy el bunduqiya

سيارات متصادمة
sayyarat mutasadima

غزل البنات
ghazl el banat

السرك
es-sirk

دراجة بهلوانية
darraja bahlawaniya

مُتلاعب
mutala"eb

بهلاوانات
bahlawanat

أرجوحة
arjooha

مشي الحبل
mashi el habl

عصا الإتزان
"asa el ittizan

حبل
habl

سلم حبلي
sullam habli

شبكة
shabaka

أرنب
arnab

قبعة عالية
quba"a "aliya

مروض
murawwed

إطار
itar

كلب
kalb

ربطة فراشية
rabta farashiyya

جوقة
jawqa

مروضة الجياد
murawwidat el jiyad

مهرج
muharrej

Arabic alphabet and word list

In the list on the opposite page you will find all the words in this book in the alphabetical order of the English words. Next to each English word is the number of the page on which it appears, and the Arabic for that word written in Roman letters to show you how to pronounce it. The Arabic words written in Arabic letters are shown on the right. Remember, Arabic is read from right to left.

There are twenty-eight letters in the Arabic alphabet. These are mostly consonants as the vowel sounds (e.g. 'a' or 'u') are shown by signs called *harakat* above or below the letters.
Here are the *harakat* for the vowel sounds:
ˊ *fatha* (a short line above the word) This gives an 'a' sound pronounced as in 'sun'.
ˏ *damma* This gives the 'u' sound pronounced as in 'soot'.
ˎ *kasra* (a short line below the word) This gives the 'i' sound pronounced as in 'sit'.

There are two other *harakat*:
˚ *sukoon* to show there is no vowel sound
— *shadda* for stressing the letter sound

Arabic alphabet

Name of letter	Letter	Sound	Pronunciation
alif	أ	a	as in 'father'
ba	ب	b	as in 'bag'
ta	ت	t	as in 'tag'
tha	ث	th	as in 'north'
jeem	ج	j	as in 'jeans'
ha	ح	h	An 'h' sound made in your throat with a lot of air. You need to hear an Arabic speaker pronounce this.
kha	خ	kh	like the 'ch' sound in 'loch'
dal	د	d	as in 'dog'
dhal	ذ	dh	as 'th' in 'then'
ra	ر	r	as in 'rag'
zein	ز	z	as in 'zoo'
seen	س	s	as in 'sun'
sheen	ش	sh	as in 'sheep'
sad	ص	s	a strong 's' as in 'song'
dad	ض	dd	a strong 'd' like the 'd' in 'don't'
ta	ط	tt	a strong 't' like the t in 'ton'
za	ظ	th	as 'th' in 'thus'
ayn	ع	"a	There is no letter to represent this sound in English. You need to ask an Arabic speaker how to say it.
ghayn	غ	gh	like the 'r' sound in French
fa	ف	f	as in 'father'
qaf	ق	q	A strong 'k' sound made at the back of your throat.
kaf	ك	k	as in 'kitty'
lam	ل	l	as in 'lemon'
meem	م	m	as in 'mouse'
noon	ن	n	as in 'nose'
ha	ه	h	as in 'his'
waw	و	w	as in 'wish'
ya	ي	y	as in 'yellow'

There is also the ء *hamza* (shown as a ' sign in this book) which can appear on its own or with an *alif* to make the following vowel sounds:

ء on its own, the *hamza* indicates a break in the word

أ with a *fatha* pronounced as the 'u' in 'utter'

أ with a *damma* pronounced as the 'u' in 'bull'

إ with a *kasra* pronounced as the 'i' in 'if'

57

59

60

popcorn, 54	fushar	فشار
potatoes, 35	batata	بطاطا
present, 47	hadiyya	هدية
puddle, 17	burreika	بريكة
pull, 43	shadd	شد
pumpkin, 35	qar"	قرع
puppets, 15	"ara'es	عرائس
puppy, 49	jaru	جرو
purple, 52	banafsaji	بنفسجي
purse, 35	haqibat yad	حقيبة يد
push, 43	daf"	دفع
R		
rabbit, 49, 55	arnab	أرنب
race, 50	sibaq er-rakd	سباق الركض
racing car, 15	sayyarat sibaq	سيارة سباق
racket, 50	madrab	مضرب
radiator, 5	radiatur	راديتير
radio, 4	radio	راديو
railway cars, 20	"arabat en-naql	عربات النقل
railway station, 20	mahatat el qitar	محطة القطار
rain, 48	matar	مطر
rainbow, 48	qaws quzah	قوس قزح
rake, 9	musht	مشط
raspberry, 33	toot	توت
read, 43	qira'a	قراءة
recorder, 14	zummara	زمارة
rectangle, 52	mustateel	مستطيل
red, 52	ahmar	أحمر
refrigerator, 6	thallaja	ثلاجة
reindeer, 47	ayl	أيل
rhinoceros, 19	karkadan	كركدن
ribbon, 32	wishah	وشاح
rice, 37	arruz	أرز
riding, 51	furusiyya	فروسية
rifle range, 54	ramy el bunduqiya	رمي البندقية
right, 45	yameen	يمين
ring, 14	khatem	خاتم
ring master, 55	murawwed	مروض
ring toss, 54	halaqaat	حلقات
river, 22	nahr	نهر
road, 22	tareeq	طريق
robot, 14	insan alee	إنسان آلي
rocket, 15	sarookh	صاروخ
rocking horse, 15	hisan hazzaz	حصان هزاز
rocks, 23	sukhoor	صخور
roller blades, 16	ahthiyat tazzalluj	أحذية تزلج
roller coaster, 54	jibal roosiyya	جبال روسية
rolls, 36	aqras khubz	أقراص خبز
roof, 12	saqf	سقف
rooster, 24	deek	ديك
rope, 27	habl	حبل
rope ladder, 55	sullam habli	سلم حبلي
rowing, 50	tajdeef	تجديف
rowboat, 27	zawraq	زورق
rug, 5	bisata	بساطة
rugby, 50	rugby	رغبي
ruler, 28	mistara	مسطرة
run, 43	rakd	ركض
runway, 21	mudarraj	مدرج
S		
saddle, 25	sarj	سرج
sailing, 50	ibhar shira"i	إبحار شراعي
sailboat, 15, 26	markab shira"i	مركب شراعي
sailor, 26	bahhar	بحار
salad, 37	salata	سلطة
salami, 33	sujuq	سجق
salt, 36	malh	ملح
sandals, 39	sandal	صندل
sandcastle, 26	qal"a ramliya	قلعة رملية
sandpaper, 10	waraq zujaj	ورق زجاج
sandpit, 16	hawd raml	حوض رمل
sandwich, 33	shateera	شطيرة
Santa Claus, 47	baba nowel	بابا نويل
Saturday, 46	es-sabt	السبت
saucepans, 6	tanaajer	طناجر
saucers, 7	suhoun sagheera	صحون صغيرة
sausage, 33	naqaneq	نقانق
saw, 10	munshar	منشار
sawdust, 10	nishara	نشارة
scales, 35	mizan	ميزان
scarecrow, 25	fazza"a	فزاعة
scarf, 39	lafha	لفحة
school, 12, 28	madrasa	مدرسة
scissors, 28	miqass	مقص
screwdriver, 10	mafak	مفك
screws, 10	baraghi sagheera	براغي صغيرة
sea, 26	bahr	بحر
seagull, 26	nawras	نورس
seal, 19	faqama	فقمة
seaside, 26	shate'	شاطيء
seasons, 48	fusool	فصول
seaweed, 27	tahaleb	طحالب
seeds, 8	bizr	بزر
seesaw, 17	zahlouka	زحلوقة
seven, 53	sab"a	سبعة (٧)
seventeen, 53	sab"ata "ashar	سبعة عشر (١٧)
sew, 43	khiyata	خياطة
shapes, 52	ashkal	أشكال
shark, 19	samak qirsh	سمك قرش
shavings, 10	nijara	نجارة
shed, 8	kukh	كوخ
sheep, 25	khirfan	خرفان
sheepdog, 24	kalb er-ra"i	كلب الراعي
sheet, 5	sharshaf	شرشف
shell, 26	sadafa	صدفة
sherpherdess, 25	ra"iya	راعية
ship, 27	safeena	سفينة
shirt, 39	qamees	قميص
shoelace, 39	rabbat	رباط
shoes, 39	ahthiya	أحذية
short, 45	qaseer	قصير
shorts, 39	sirwal qaseer	سروال قصير
shoulders, 38	katef	كتف
shovel, 8, 26	majrafa	مجرفة
shower, 4	doosh	دوش
signals, 13, 20	isharat daw'iya	إشارات ضوئية
signpost, 22	"amood el ittijahat	عمود الإتجاهات
sing, 43	ghina'	غناء
singers, 40	mughani	مغني
sink, 4, 6	maghsaleh	مغسلة
sister, 41	ukht	أخت
sit, 43	juloos	جلوس
six, 53	sitta	ستة (٦)
sixteen, 53	sittata "ashar	ستة عشر (١٦)
skateboard, 17	lawhat tazzaluj	لوحة تزلج
ski pole, 51	"asa tazalluj	عصا تزلج
skiing, 51	tazalluj "ala eth-thalj	تزلج على الثلج
skip, 43	qafz bil habl	قفز بالحبل
skirt, 39	tannoura	تنورة
skis, 51	mazalej	مزالج

63

First published in 2004 by Usborne Publishing Ltd, Usborne House, 83-85 Saffron Hill, London EC1N 8RT, England. www.usborne.com. Based on a previous title first published in 1979 and revised in 1995. Copyright © 2003, 1995, 1979 Usborne Publishing Ltd. This American edition published in 2004. AE

Printed in Italy.

11-05RC